Meet Kitty & her Cat Crew

Kitty

Kitty has special powers but is she ready to be a superhero just like her mum?

Luckily Kitty's Cat Crew have faith in her and show Kitty the hero that lies within!

Pumpkin

A stray ginger kitten who is utterly devoted to Kitty.

Figaro

Excitable and ready for adventure, Figaro knows
the neighbourhood like the back of his paw.

Pixie

Pixie has a nose for trouble
and a very active imagination!

Katsumi

Sleek and sophisticated,
Katsumi is quick to call Kitty
at the first sign of trouble.

For Henry and his favourite cats, Max and Evie. - P.H.

For Clare and Lizzie, the best team! - J.L.

OXFORD
UNIVERSITY PRESS

Great Clarendon Street, Oxford OX2 6DP

Oxford University Press is a department of the University of Oxford.
It furthers the University's objective of excellence in research, scholarship, and
education by publishing worldwide. Oxford is a registered trade mark of Oxford
University Press in the UK and in certain other countries

Text copyright © Paula Harrison 2020
Illustrations copyright © Jenny Løvlie 2020

The moral rights of the author/illustrator have been asserted
Database right Oxford University Press (maker)

First published 2020

British Library Cataloguing in Publication Data

Data available

ISBN: 978-0-19-277169-8

1 3 5 7 9 10 8 6 4 2

Printed in China

Paper used in the production of this book is a natural,
recyclable product made from wood grown in sustainable forests.
The manufacturing process conforms to the environmental
regulations of the country of origin.

Kitty

and the
Great Lantern Race

OXFORD

UNIVERSITY PRESS

Chapter 1

Kitty cut out two pointy cat ears and carefully stuck them on to her paper lantern. She smiled, lifting the lantern up by its handle. Tomorrow evening the whole of Hallam City would celebrate the Festival of Light.

There would be a huge parade through the city streets with a beautiful firework display at the end.

All around the classroom, children were making different sorts of lanterns. Each one would have a candle-shaped

light bulb placed inside. Kitty couldn't wait to see them all shine in the dark like a mass of twinkling stars. She had made her lantern look like a cat's face using black and white paper, and long whiskers made from black straws.

It looked a little bit like her cat friend, Figaro!

Kitty had a special reason for making a cat-shaped lantern. She had amazing cat-like superpowers and she was training to be a real superhero. She often went out in the moonlight to have adventures with her cat crew, leaping and somersaulting across the city roofs. Kitty loved feeling her special powers tingling inside her. She also loved being with her cat friends, especially Pumpkin, the roly-poly ginger kitten

who slept on her
bed every night.

Emily, who sat
opposite Kitty in class,
tapped her on the arm.
'Look, Kitty! Do you like my butterfly?'
She showed Kitty her lantern, which
had bright purple wings edged with
silver sparkles, and delicate green
antennae.

'That looks beautiful!' Kitty said,
admiringly.

Emily beamed. 'I can't wait till

tomorrow. The lantern parade is going to be amazing. My mum and dad are coming to watch with my Aunty Sarah.'

Kitty's heart sank a little as she remembered that her parents wouldn't be there. Her mum, who was a superhero herself, would be working and her dad didn't want to keep her little brother, Max, up too late. But at least she would be with her school friends and maybe the cat crew would come to watch too!

'It's going to be brilliant!' she

agreed. 'I wonder who will win the prize this year.'

'I hope it's someone from our class,' said Emily.

Every school in Hallam City took part in the lantern parade and, at the end, there was a prize for the best lantern. This year, the prize would be a magnificent crown decorated with a gleaming golden star. Their teacher, Mrs Phillips, had brought the crown in to show them and it was standing on her desk at the front of the classroom, glittering in the sunlight. Everyone had worked extra hard on their lanterns once they'd seen how beautiful it was.

Mrs Phillips clapped her hands. 'The lanterns look wonderful, everyone! You can take them home with you today, but don't forget to bring them along to the festival tomorrow night.'

Kitty picked up her lantern by its handle and smiled. She couldn't wait to show her lamp to her family and all her cat friends.

When darkness fell, Kitty switched on the candle light bulb inside her

lantern and placed it on her
bedroom windowsill. She hoped
lots of the cat crew would visit
tonight. Then she could tell them

all about the Festival of Light and ask them if they'd like to watch her in the lantern parade.

She watched the moon rise, casting a silvery glow over the roofs of the houses. The sky darkened and the swaying tree branches sent shadows dancing across the walls. Hundreds of

stars began to appear, glittering like tiny diamonds.

Pumpkin, who was curled up on Kitty's bed, gave a huge yawn.

'Aren't you tired yet, Kitty?'

'Not yet!' Kitty smiled. 'Do you think Figaro and the others will come to see us tonight?'

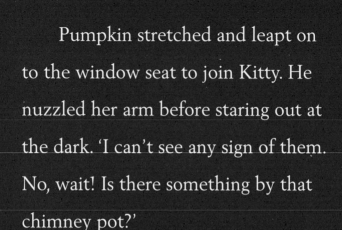

Pumpkin stretched and leapt on
to the window seat to join Kitty. He
nuzzled her arm before staring out at
the dark. 'I can't see any sign of them.
No, wait! Is there something by that
chimney pot?'

Kitty opened the window a
little and the night breeze ruffled the
curtains. Her cat-like superpowers

rushed through her body, making her
skin tingle. Using her special night-time
vision and super hearing, she peered
into the dark. Suddenly everything
looked sharp and clear, and she could
hear dozens of tiny sounds, from a
car whooshing past to a tiny moth
fluttering beside a streetlamp.

She turned her attention to the

distant rooftops. A black cat with a white face and paws sprang jauntily along the ridge of a roof. Scampering in front of him was a fluffy white cat with bright green eyes.

'Figaro and Pixie are coming!' she told Pumpkin, and the ginger kitten's stripy tail swished excitedly.

'Good evening, Kitty!'

called Figaro, when he reached her windowsill. 'Well, that is a fine-looking lantern. Did you make it yourself?'

'Yes, I did! It's for the Festival of Light tomorrow.' Kitty explained all about the lantern parade and the fireworks. 'So I hoped you might come and watch me from a nearby rooftop.'

'I didn't know there would be fireworks.' Pumpkin trembled and put one paw to his cheek.

'Maybe I should stay here instead . . .'

'I don't like them either. They make such horrible bangs and crashes!' Pixie agreed. 'Don't worry, Pumpkin. I'll stay here and look after you.'

'Fireworks are such a nuisance!' said Figaro, twirling his whiskers. 'Perhaps I will also stay behind. But I hope you have a wonderful time in the parade, Kitty. Maybe your lantern will win that amazing prize!'

Kitty swallowed her disappointment. She should have remembered that lots of cats hated fireworks. But at least this way Pumpkin would have friends around to look after him. 'I'll tell you all about it when I get back,' she promised. 'I think it'll be a night to remember!'

Chapter 2

Kitty fizzed with excitement the following evening as she joined the crowds of children taking part in the parade. The full moon shone brightly and the streets were full of people. Long gold and red streamers hung

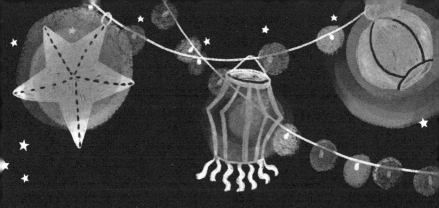

between the lampposts and glowing
lamps dangled from the trees like
magical golden fruit. A frosty breeze
blew gently along the road and Kitty
zipped her coat up tight.

Emily linked arms with Kitty.
'There are so many people here!
And look at all these lanterns.'

Kitty spotted a train lantern
and a unicorn one with a shiny horn.

There are so many different ones.' She smiled at her friend. 'But I still think your butterfly lantern is the best.'

Mrs Phillips called everyone over and the parade began. Everyone lit their lanterns and the crowd moved forward

together, their lights bobbing like one enormous, sparkly caterpillar. Spectators lined the streets, clapping as the troop of children went past.

Kitty beamed. It was wonderful to be part of something so spectacular.

She looked around at all the people
and the lights. She wanted to be able
to describe it all to Pumpkin, Pixie and
Figaro when she got home.

A movement on a nearby rooftop
caught her eye. She
glanced up and saw
a black shape darting
past a chimney pot.
Moonlight winked
on a nearby
satellite dish.

When Kitty looked at the rooftop
again, the figure was gone.

The parade moved on, reaching a
bend in the road, and the streamers on
the lampposts fluttered in the breeze.

'My watch is missing!' shouted a
man in the crowd.

Kitty looked over at once. A grey-
haired man was staring at his arm in

shock. He checked his pockets before searching the ground around his feet. 'Where is it?' he cried. 'I felt something brush against my arm and then it was gone!'

'Maybe the strap broke and it fell off,' said the man next to him.

The grey-haired man shook his head vigorously. 'No, I'm sure it didn't! I only bought it last week and the strap is very strong. I don't understand it!'

Kitty frowned. It seemed very odd that someone's watch would disappear like that. As the parade moved on, she watched the crowd carefully. Her night vision picked up every tiny movement in the darkness and she used her super hearing to focus on any strange sounds.

She glimpsed a shadowy figure slipping past a shop doorway. Kitty tried to keep track of the shadow, but it seemed to melt away into the mass of people and, a moment later, a woman in a furry white coat gave a terrible shriek. 'My ruby necklace . . . it's gone!'

Kitty dashed through the crowd. 'What happened?' she asked the lady. 'Could the necklace have fallen off?'

'I don't think so.' The woman clutched her neck. 'I felt something . . . like a brush of fur against my throat.

Then I looked down and my precious
string of red rubies was gone!'

Kitty looked around quickly.
Everyone standing close to the lady
looked just as confused as she did.

'My husband gave me that necklace when we got married so it's very precious to me.' Tears pricked the woman's eyes. 'Who could have done such a horrible thing?'

Kitty held her lantern tightly. There was something suspicious about all this. The watch and the ruby necklace had both disappeared very suddenly, and that made her think it wasn't an accident. But who had taken them . . . and how?

Kitty knew she wanted to help. She was a superhero-in-training after all! Her stomach felt strange, as if there were moths fluttering inside her. Was this really a good idea? She didn't have any of her cat crew to help her this time. Pumpkin and the others were far away at home. She would be investigating the missing watch and necklace all by herself. How would she manage all alone?

She took a deep breath. Her superhero skills were needed right now, so she had to find a way! She remembered what her mum had

told her the first time she went on a
moonlight adventure: *Don't let fear hold
you back. You're braver than you think!*
She just had to do her best.

She hurried back to Emily's side.

'A lady's necklace has vanished and I
have to go and help,' she told her friend.
'Could you look after my lantern?'

'Course I can!' Emily took the cat
lantern. 'Will you be all right?'

Kitty smiled bravely. 'Don't worry
about me! I'm going to look around and
see what I can find out.'

'Good luck!' said Emily, her eyes
wide.

Kitty slipped away from the crowd
and into the shadows. Hiding behind a
tree, she threw off her coat to reveal her

cat superhero outfit
underneath. Her cape
unfurled in the night breeze. She
was glad she'd put it on before
coming out tonight. It was always
good to be prepared!

Pulling her superhero
mask out of her pocket,
she put it on and looked
around in the gloom.

Was the shadowy figure she'd spotted connected to the disappearing watch and necklace? She didn't know for sure, but if she was right someone could be stealing people's belongings while they were busy watching the lantern parade.

If that was true, it had to be someone very sneaky who could slip in and out of the crowd without anyone noticing. She had to stop them before they stole even more valuables.

Kitty felt a rush of energy.

She darted over to a streetlight and shinned up the post to get a better view. From here, she could see over the heads of the crowd. The parade was moving on and dozens of lanterns bobbed up and down in the darkness. The spectators clapped and the red and gold streamers flapped in the wind.

Kitty frowned. Where was that strange figure?

Suddenly, she spotted a pair of amber eyes watching her from behind a postbox on the other side of the street. A black mask covered the figure's face but her sharp eyes were full of mischief. Before Kitty could get a better look the shadowy figure moved on, slipping through the crowd and dodging round lampposts.

Kitty's skin tingled. She had a funny feeling deep down that she had just found the jewel thief!

Chapter 3

Kitty leapt down from the lamppost, landing gracefully on the pavement. The escaping thief darted through the crowd, jumping over litter bins. Kitty chased her down the street, her superpowers tingling through her body. The robber was still a long way ahead but Kitty was sure she could catch her.

The thief glanced around, her eyes glinting. She laughed when she saw Kitty chasing her. Then she swooped into the crowd and snatched a handbag from a lady's arm, before dodging behind the next lamppost. The lady clutched her shoulder and looked around in alarm.

'Hey!' cried Kitty. 'Give that back.'

The thief took no notice of Kitty.

Slippery as
a shadow, she
vanished into
the crowd and
appeared again
on the opposite
side of the road.
Kitty ran even
faster. Leaping on to a
bench, she grabbed hold of a tree
branch and used it to swing herself
right across the street. She landed
neatly and kept on running. The thief

was just ahead, dodging around a litter
bin. Then she ducked behind a line of
people and disappeared again.

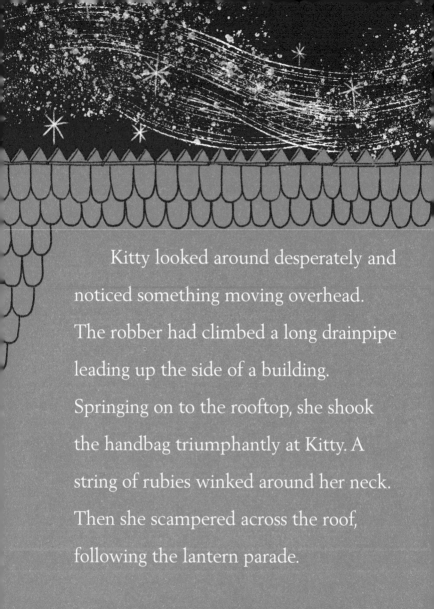

Kitty looked around desperately and noticed something moving overhead. The robber had climbed a long drainpipe leading up the side of a building. Springing on to the rooftop, she shook the handbag triumphantly at Kitty. A string of rubies winked around her neck. Then she scampered across the roof, following the lantern parade.

Kitty pulled herself skilfully up
the drainpipe, one hand after the other.
There was something really strange
about this thief. She was very small and
fast, and she seemed used to heights. She
certainly didn't seem to care how many
people she robbed. Kitty was determined
to catch the crook before she ruined the
whole festival.

The icy wind spun across the rooftop, making Kitty's cape swirl. She ran lightly along the ridge of the roof, following the thief as she jumped the narrow gap between two buildings. Below them, the parade went on moving and the streets were full of noise and laughter.

Kitty felt very alone on the rooftop. She thought of all the times her friends had helped her and cheered her on. She wished she had Figaro or Pixie or any of her cat crew to keep her company.

She took a deep breath. There
must be a way to outsmart this villain.
They might be planning to swoop down
to the street and rob someone else in
the crowd. Maybe she could take a
shortcut and catch the robber as she
returned to the rooftop.

Kitty hid behind a chimney pot.
Then, when she was sure the thief
wasn't looking, she climbed from a
window ledge to the ground. Racing
along the street, she climbed back to
the rooftop a little further on. If this

worked, she could catch the robber by surprise! She peered down at the crowd, expecting to see the shadowy figure.

The crowd went on clapping. People's voices drifted up from the street below. Kitty caught sight of Emily carrying the butterfly and cat lanterns. She balanced at the edge of the roof, watching and waiting.

The parade was moving towards a brightly lit platform at the end of the street. The Mayor of Hallam City stood

waiting there, dressed
in her best clothes. Kitty
used her special vision to look
more closely. The Mayor was holding
the golden crown—the prize for the
best lantern—and the beautiful star
decoration gleamed in the light.

It would be given out during a special ceremony at the end of the parade.

A shadow moved on a rooftop right beside the platform. Kitty felt a flutter of alarm. How had the thief got so far without her noticing?

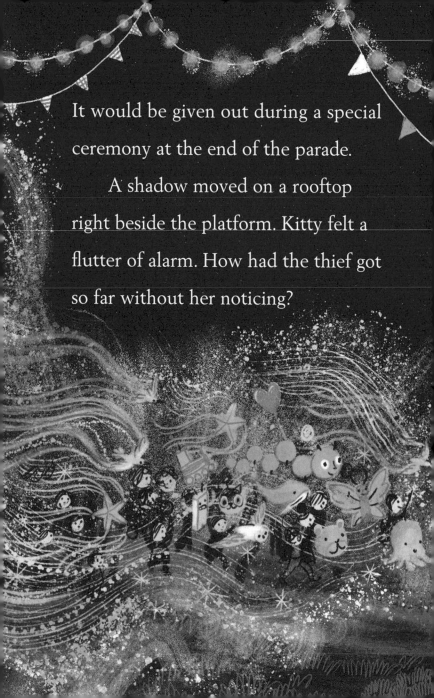

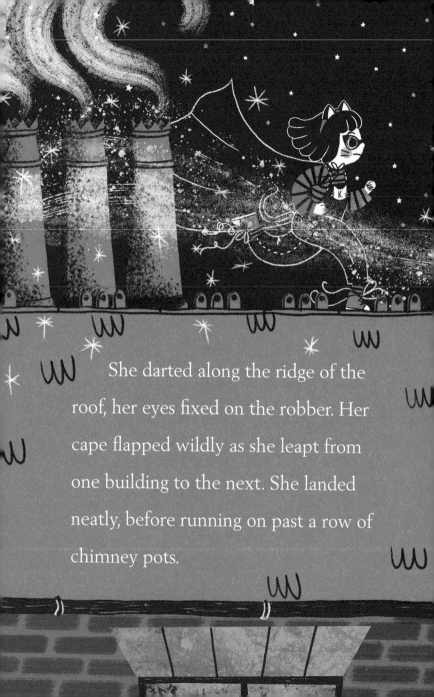

She darted along the ridge of the
roof, her eyes fixed on the robber. Her
cape flapped wildly as she leapt from
one building to the next. She landed
neatly, before running on past a row of
chimney pots.

The thief swung down a nearby drainpipe and made a graceful leap to the ground. Then she crept closer to the stage, prowling in and out of the shadows. Everyone in the crowd was smiling at the children in the lantern parade. None of them had seen the shadowy figure moving towards the platform.

The thief's gaze was fixed on the Mayor. Kitty's heart sank. She must be after the golden crown!

With a burst of energy, Kitty ran faster than ever. The wind whistled past her ears and her cape streamed out behind her. She jumped from rooftop to rooftop. Then she swung down a drainpipe before dropping to the ground.

The thief crept up the platform

steps. Her sharp amber eyes spotted Kitty at the edge of the crowd and she laughed.

'Stop!' cried Kitty. 'You can't take the prize. You'll ruin the whole festival!' But her voice was lost among the clapping and cheering of the crowd.

The robber tiptoed up behind the Mayor and, for a second, Kitty got a clear view of the shadowy figure. There was something very familiar about her graceful movements and her pricked-up ears. Then the thief snatched the crown from the Mayor's fingers, before leaping off the platform and disappearing down an alleyway.

The Mayor stared down at her empty hand in surprise. A murmur of shock swept across the crowd.

'What happened to the crown?' asked a woman close to Kitty.

'I think someone took it!' gasped the man next to her.

The parade came to a stop and the children with the lanterns bumped into each other. Some of them pointed to the Mayor as they passed on the bad news about the missing crown. A small boy with a dinosaur lantern burst into tears.

'It's not just the crown that's vanished,' one lady called out. 'That thief took my handbag too!'

'And my watch!' shouted a man. 'Maybe there's a whole gang of robbers here tonight.'

The buzz of the crowd grew louder and Kitty's school teacher climbed the steps to the platform and talked hurriedly to the Mayor. At last, the Mayor stepped forward and held up her hand for quiet. 'Please, everyone, stay calm! I don't know what's happening to our lovely Festival but I will do my best to find out.'

Kitty's heart thumped. None of

them had really seen the robber except for her. She had to find that thief and get the crown back! She peered down the alley where the crook had vanished. Then she straightened her superhero mask before running on into the dark.

Chapter 4

Kitty raced down the alley.
The noise of the crowd faded as she
ran further away from the festival.
She stopped at a corner and listened
carefully for any tiny sounds. The wind
whistled gently down the moonlit street

and there was the distant hoot of an owl. A cluster of fallen leaves danced in the night breeze.

Quick footsteps came from another alley not far away. Kitty followed the faint sound, hoping it was the thief. She zig-zagged through the maze of streets and alleys. Every now and then, the footsteps stopped and Kitty paused too. It would be easier to catch the thief if she didn't know she was being followed.

The next alley opened into a wide

road full of shops and restaurants.
Moonlight glinted like frost on the shop
windows. A sign in a café window read
*Delicious soups and noodles served all
day*. The Hallam Wonder Tower, the
highest building in the whole city, rose
into the night like a vast stone giant.

Kitty waited and waited, but
there were no more footsteps. Had
the thief realized she was following?

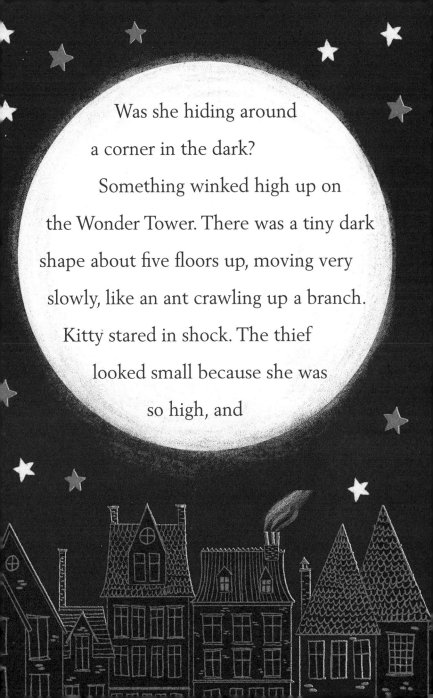

Was she hiding around
a corner in the dark?
Something winked high up on
the Wonder Tower. There was a tiny dark
shape about five floors up, moving very
slowly, like an ant crawling up a branch.
Kitty stared in shock. The thief
looked small because she was
so high, and

the glinting light was the star on

the golden crown shining in the

moonlight.

Kitty's heart fluttered.

She knew her superpowers

would help her . . . but

did she really want to go

all the way up there?

The Wonder Tower was

enormous. It had a place

to eat at the top called

the Cloud Restaurant

and, above that, a metal

radio mast jutted into the sky. Kitty could see the top of the mast with its flashing red light that warned away aeroplanes.

She shivered. Maybe the tower was too high even for someone with special powers. But there were stolen handbags and necklaces that had to be taken back to their owners . . . and how could the lantern competition go ahead with no prize? She thought of the disappointed faces of her classmates. Hurrying to the bottom of the tower, she began to climb.

She had to work hard to find handholds and footholds in the smooth stone building and the higher she went, the stronger the wind became. She looked up just as the thief disappeared through an open window on the sixth floor. She must be planning to hide somewhere inside.

Kitty climbed to the sixth floor and dropped through the same window. She was standing on a staircase with long flights of steps leading up and down. Quick footsteps sounded overhead.

Kitty followed the steps upwards, treading as quietly as she could.

The stairs wound on and on. Kitty counted the floors . . . nine, ten, eleven . . . twenty-four, twenty-five, twenty-six . . . She lost count around the fortieth floor, but a minute later she found herself on the final set of steps. A magnificent set of doors, with the name

Cloud
Restaurant

in big gold letters, stood at the top.

Kitty hesitated. The thief must

have gone inside. She crept a little closer.

There was a sudden whirring sound from inside the restaurant. Kitty warily opened the door and spotted an elegant black cat sitting on a stool at the counter. Her long tail flicked as she drank from a tall glass through a stripy red straw. The festival crown, the handbag and all the other loot lay on the counter top.

Kitty stopped a gasp. So the thief was a cat! That was why she'd climbed buildings so easily and leapt so gracefully from one roof to the next. Kitty had to admit that the cat burglar was the most nimble creature she'd ever seen, and one of the sneakiest too. But how dare she sit there relaxing after spoiling the parade!

Creeping up silently, Kitty dived at the thief and grabbed her before she could escape.

The robber jumped in surprise and

her drink spurted all over the counter.

'Hey, what's going on? Who are you?'

'I'm Kitty and I've come to take back all the things you stole!' said Kitty. 'You should be ashamed of yourself.' She spun the thief round to face her and pulled off the cat's mask. Underneath were a set of elegant whiskers, a cute black nose and mischievous amber eyes.

'You caught me! No one's ever done that before. My name's Dodger, by the way!' The cat grinned and held out a furry black paw. Her tail swayed gracefully.

Kitty let go of her, frowning. This cat didn't seem bothered by being caught at all. Why didn't she look cross or even guilty?

Dodger lifted her glass again and slurped through the stripy straw. 'I can make you some of this drink if you like, Kitty. Mango and fish smoothie is my favourite!'

Kitty shook her head. This wasn't going the way she'd expected. 'Why are you here? Are you stealing from the restaurant?'

'I live here! The cook lets me sleep under the tables and sometimes the customers give me their chicken or fish to eat. I love being high up. It makes me feel like I could do anything!' Dodger scampered over to the window and waved her paw at the bright full moon smiling down on the city below. 'See that view? It's the best in the city!'

Kitty followed her to the window. The whole of Hallam city was spread out below them in a carpet of little twinkling lights. Kitty could just about make out the park near her house and the clock tower where she'd first met Pumpkin. The whole city had a magical silvery look in the moonlight.

'Hey, you should come and live here with me!' Dodger carried on. 'It's brilliant here and you have all the right cat skills to be part of my crew.'

'You're right—it's amazing here,' Kitty agreed. 'But I already have a cat crew and we do things to help people not hurt them.'

Dodger snorted. 'That sounds really boring!'

'It's not boring—it's important work. I would never steal anything.

Don't you realize how many people you've upset this evening?'

Dodger flicked her tail. 'What do you mean? I was only having fun.'

'It's not fun to steal other people's things,' said Kitty sternly. 'The lady with the ruby necklace said her husband gave her those jewels on the day they got married. They were very special to her.'

Dodger looked a little downcast. Then her amber eyes gleamed. 'But how about this?' She bounded back to the counter and put the festival crown on her head. 'This didn't really belong to anyone and see how great it looks on me!' The crown slipped sideways over her velvety-black ear.

Kitty wanted to laugh for a moment but she stopped herself. 'Taking that crown was the worst thing you did! It was supposed to be the prize at the end of the festival. Lots of children will be disappointed that it's gone.'

'That's stupid! I think you're just trying to ruin all my fun,' cried Dodger, shooting Kitty a cross look. Then she snatched up all her loot and raced out of the restaurant doors.

Kitty dashed after her, but by the time she reached the stairs the slippery cat thief was gone.

Chapter 5

Kitty rushed down the steps, looking for Dodger. Halfway down she stopped and listened, but everywhere was silent. How had Dodger disappeared so fast?

It took a long time to reach the

bottom floor and, just as she got there, the elevator door slid closed. Dodger must have come down in the lift before escaping into the night.

Kitty opened a window and climbed out on to the pavement. A cloud hid the moon and the street grew darker. Kitty looked along the empty road, frowning. A feeling deep down inside made her follow the alleyway leading back to the festival.

All the chatter and laughter had disappeared from the crowded streets.

The children in the lantern parade were waiting close to the Mayor's platform. They held their lanterns by their sides, their shoulders slumped. A group of teachers had gathered on the stage to talk to the Mayor.

A shadow jumped out at Kitty as she reached the end of the alleyway.

'I know you're following me! Have you come to spoil my fun again?' Dodger scowled. The golden crown still sat lopsided on her head.

'Dodger, you've got to listen to

me!' said Kitty. 'Stealing things isn't fun—it just makes everyone sad. See that lady over there? She's the one whose handbag you took.'

Dodger looked at the lady who was wiping a tear from her eye.

'And look at my friends!' Kitty went on. 'They spent a long time making their lanterns and they were having a wonderful time till the prize was taken away.'

Kitty's classmates were looking round worriedly, as if they were afraid the thief might return any moment.

'Does it really look like they're having fun now?' Kitty demanded.

Dodger stared at them and a guilty look spread across her face. 'I guess not! I'm sorry, Kitty. When I left the tower tonight I just wanted an adventure so I set myself a challenge to steal the festival prize. I *love* to test my awesome cat burglar skills!' She preened her smooth black fur. 'Then when I got here and saw the crowd it seemed funny to take the other things too while no one was looking. I didn't think I was hurting anyone.'

'Maybe we can put everything

right together,' suggested Kitty.

Dodger stroked her long whiskers. 'All right then! But how do we do that?'

'All we have to do is give back what you took . . . and if we use our cat-like skills it will be just as fun,' explained Kitty. 'Let's see which of us can return the valuables to their owners the quickest.'

Dodger's eyes gleamed. 'I accept your challenge! I know I'm bound to be the winner.'

Kitty took the lady's handbag and

the man's watch and bounded down the street. Dodger scampered after her with the ruby necklace and the golden crown.

'Last one to finish is a slow-poke cat!' Dodger called. 'Oh . . . and you have to put each thing back without anyone seeing.'

'You're on!' Kitty called back. Then she slipped through the crowd and hung the stolen handbag back on to the lady's shoulder.

Dodger climbed nimbly up a

lamppost and spotted the
woman with the ruby
necklace on the other side
of the crowd. The black
cat skipped along a tree
branch, before leaping across
the street and slipping the
necklace over the lady's head.

The woman gasped and
clutched the string of rubies.

'My necklace! Where did that come from?'

'I think I saw a figure moving over there!' said the man beside her, pointing in the wrong direction.

'It's incredible!' the woman went on. 'It just appeared like magic.'

Dodger grinned and crept into the darkness of a nearby alley.

Kitty slipped the missing watch on to the wrist of the man it belonged to. She noticed Dodger sneaking on to the platform at the front of the crowd. The wily black cat left the crown on a table and disappeared again like a shadow vanishing in the moonlight.

A moment later, Dodger reappeared at Kitty's side, grinning. 'That was a lot of fun! But do you think they'll ever notice that I've put the crown back?'

Kitty smiled. The Mayor and the teachers were still busy talking to each other. None of them had noticed the prize lying on the table in the middle of the platform. Then a shout went up as one of the children spotted the crown. A murmur of excitement went around the crowd.

The prize has been found!' said a dark-haired lady. 'Isn't that amazing?'

'That's really good news,' replied the man next to her. 'I hated seeing the children disappointed.'

So I guess I'm a very good cat after all! *And* I won our competition. I knew I would be the fastest!' Dodger did a triumphant little dance and waved her tail in Kitty's face.

'Well, actually . . .' Kitty was just about to explain that she'd finished first, but then she stopped herself. She had a hunch that Dodger wouldn't be a good loser, and this way the cat thief was happy about giving back the stolen things. 'I'm very proud of you! Are you going to stay and see them give out the prize for the best lantern?'

'I don't think so.' Dodger's tail flicked restlessly. 'It's still early and there might be another adventure waiting for me somewhere!'

Kitty's forehead wrinkled. 'You won't steal anything else, will you? Don't forget how much nicer it is to make people happy.'

'Sure—I'll remember!' Dodger winked and smoothed her whiskers. 'I hope I'll see you again some time, Kitty. Come to the Cloud Restaurant if you ever want to try a mango and fish smoothie!'

'Thanks, I will! Good luck, Dodger.'
Kitty watched the graceful black cat
dart away into the crowd.

Dodger waved to her with a grin,
her amber eyes gleaming as she slipped
away down an alley.

Kitty waved back, smiling. She'd
completed a whole adventure without
the help of her cat crew. She couldn't
wait to tell her mum all about it!
Excitement fluttered in her tummy
as the Mayor walked to the front of
the platform with the golden crown.

It looked like the prize-giving was about to begin!

Chapter 6

Kitty dashed over to join her class. 'Thanks for looking after my lantern!' she said to Emily.

'That's all right!' replied Emily. 'Did you see what happened? The crown was found again after all.'

Kitty nodded, smiling to herself.

Just then, the Mayor began to speak. 'Ladies and gentlemen! I'm very pleased that our prize has been returned and a big thank you to anyone that helped get it back again. Now I'm going to announce the winner of the lantern competition.'

A murmur rippled across the crowd and everyone watched the Mayor eagerly.

'The judges have walked around the parade and looked at all the lanterns carefully,' the Mayor continued. 'There were so many brilliant ones this year and that made it very tricky, but we've decided that the winner is . . . Emily Sanchez with her butterfly lantern!'

The crowd burst into applause. Kitty's whole class cheered and Emily turned red.

'Go on!' Kitty urged her friend. 'You have to go up on stage and collect your prize.'

Emily made her way up the platform steps and shook the Mayor's hand. Then she held up her purple butterfly lantern with its silver-edged wings so that everyone could see it properly.

The crowd clapped loudly and the Mayor placed the golden crown on Emily's head, saying, 'Here's your prize! Very well done for making such an imaginative and beautiful lantern.'

Kitty smiled

and cheered. She had been sure that Emily's lantern was the best one all along! She felt a tap on her shoulder. Spinning round, she found her mum right behind her. 'Mum, you made it!' she beamed. 'Look! Emily won the lantern competition.'

'That's amazing!' Mum put an arm around her shoulder. 'I'm sorry I missed the parade. Did you have a wonderful time?'

'Yes, it's been really exciting!' Kitty told her. 'The festival prize went missing and I had to chase the thief to find it.'

'Goodness! I'd love to hear all about
it,' said Mum.

Together they left the crowd and
climbed on to a nearby rooftop. The
festival streamers fluttered on the
lampposts below and the lanterns shone
brightly in the dark.

'Let's find somewhere comfortable
to sit,' said Kitty's mum. 'I think the
fireworks are about to start.'

They found a comfortable spot
beside a chimney just as the fireworks

began. Fountains of gold and silver light whooshed into the air before falling down again like glittering rain.

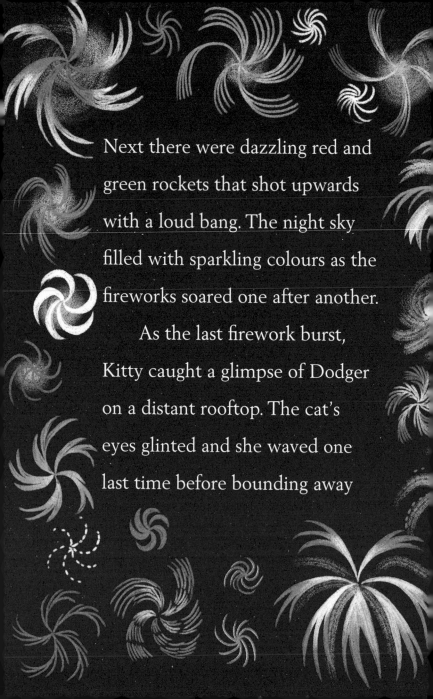

Next there were dazzling red and green rockets that shot upwards with a loud bang. The night sky filled with sparkling colours as the fireworks soared one after another.

As the last firework burst, Kitty caught a glimpse of Dodger on a distant rooftop. The cat's eyes glinted and she waved one last time before bounding away into the night.

Kitty told her mum all about Dodger and how hard she'd worked to catch the naughty cat. 'So I went all the way to the top of the Wonder Tower to talk to Dodger. She's quite a cheeky cat, but once she understood how much she'd upset everyone she gave everything back again.'

'Well done!' Mum hugged her. 'It can't have been easy all by yourself. I'm so proud of you! Would you like to go home and celebrate with some hot chocolate and marshmallow sprinkles?'

'Yes, please!' Kitty watched the last firework soar through the sky like a

cluster of shooting stars. Then she
went home with her mum, skipping
across the rooftops in the moonlight.

Back home there would be
hot chocolate and Pumpkin and her
cosy bed. Having an adventure was
amazing, but going home at the end
was even nicer!

Kitty

and the
Moonlight Rescue

Kitty

and the
Moonlight Rescue

Girl by day. Cat by night. Ready for adventure.

Written by Paula Harrison • Illustrated by Jenny Løvlie

A magical adventure
by the light of the moon.

Kitty's family is **extra special**—Mum is a
superhero and Kitty knows that one day she'll use
her special powers to be a hero too. That day comes
sooner than expected when Figaro the cat comes
to her bedroom window to ask for help.

But the world at night is a scary place—is Kitty
brave enough to step out into the darkness for a
thrilling moonlight adventure?

Kitty

and the
Tiger Treasure

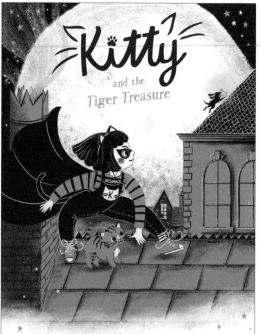

Kitty

and the
Tiger Treasure

Girl by day. Cat by night. Ready for adventure.

Written by **Paula Harrison** • *Illustrated by* **Jenny Løvlie**

A magical adventure
by the light of the moon.

Kitty can't wait to visit the museum and see the
priceless Golden Tiger Statue with her own eyes.
Legend tells that those in possession of the statue
can make their greatest wish come true . . .

Kitty takes a moonlight trip to show Pumpkin
the statue while there's no one else around, but
disaster strikes when the statue is stolen and Kitty
is accused of the crime. Will Kitty clear her name,
find the culprit, and return the precious
statue before sunrise?

Kitty

and the
Sky Garden Adventure

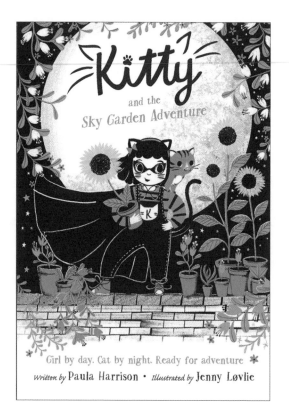

Kitty

and the
Sky Garden Adventure

Girl by day. Cat by night. Ready for adventure

Written by **Paula Harrison** • *Illustrated by* **Jenny Løvlie**

A magical adventure
by the light of the moon.

Kitty, Pumpkin, and Pixie discover a
secret sky garden on the city rooftops.

It's a **wondrous place**, filled with exotic plants
and beautiful decorations. Pixie is so excited that
she wants to tell the world about it, but the more
cats that learn of the secret garden, the wilder
it becomes. Soon Kitty has to step in to **rescue
the garden** and its beauty from those who
seem intent on destroying it.

Kitty

and the
Treetop Chase

Kitty

and the
Treetop Chase

Girl by day. Cat by night. Ready for adventure.

Written by Paula Harrison • Illustrated by Jenny Løvlie

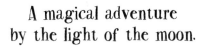

A magical adventure
by the light of the moon.

Making friends can be difficult when you feel
different from everybody else.

Luckily, Kitty's mum has set up a play date for
Kitty to meet a little boy who has **superpowers**
too. But just because you share superpowers,
doesn't mean you can instantly be friends.

Friendships take work, and in this case, it's **heroic
teamwork** and a **magical midnight feast**
that brings Kitty and her new friend together.

Super facts about Cats

Super Speed

Have you ever seen a cat make a quick escape from a dog? If so, you'll know that they can move *really* fast—up to 30mph!

Super Hearing

Cats have an incredible sense of hearing and can swivel their large ears to pinpoint even the tiniest of sounds.

Super Reflexes

Have you ever heard the saying 'cats always land on their feet'? People say this because cats have amazing reflexes. If a cat is falling, they can sense quickly how to move their bodies into the right position to land safely.

Super Leaps

A cat can jump over eight feet high
in a single leap, this is due to its powerful
back leg muscles.

Super Vision

Cats have amazing night-time vision. Their
incredible ability to see in low light allows them
to hunt for prey when it's dark outside.

Super Smell

Cats have a very powerful sense of smell,
14 times stronger than a human's. Did you know
that the pattern of ridges on each cat's nose
is as unique as a human's fingerprint?

About the author

Paula Harrison

Before launching a successful writing career,
Paula was a primary school teacher. Her years teaching
taught her what children like in stories and how
they respond to humour and suspense. She went on
to put her experience to good use, writing many
successful stories for young readers.

About the illustrator

Jenny Løvlie

Jenny is a Norwegian illustrator, designer,
creative, foodie and bird enthusiast. She is fascinated
by the strong bond between humans and animals and
loves using bold colours and shapes in her work.

Love Kitty?
Why not try these too . . .